REVENGE OF THE SKULL SPIDERS

By Ryder Windham

SCHOLASTIC

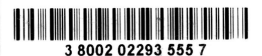

Scholastic Children's Books
Euston House,
24 Eversholt Street,
London NW1 1DB, UK

A division of Scholastic Ltd
London ~ New York ~ Toronto ~ Sydney ~ Auckland
Mexico City ~ New Delhi ~ Hong Kong

This book was first published in the US in 2015 by Scholastic Inc.
Published in the UK by Scholastic Ltd, 2016

ISBN 978 1407 16225 6

Printed and bound by CPI Group (UK) Ltd, Croydon, CR0 4YY

2 4 6 8 10 9 7 5 3 1

Papers used by Scholastic Children's Books are made from woods grown in sustainable forests.

www.scholastic.co.uk

FSC www.fsc.org MIX Paper from responsible sources FSC® C020471

CHAPTER 1

THE PROTECTORS ASSEMBLE

Vizuna, the Protector of Jungle on the island Okoto, climbed quickly to the top of a tall tree at the edge of the jungle so he would have a better view of the battle on the bridge. The bridge was a monumental structure with towering supports and an observation deck at its centre, and it extended over a deep, wide chasm to the City of the Mask Makers. Hoping to stay out of sight, he concealed himself behind the tree's broad leaves, and coiled his sensor tail around a thick branch so he wouldn't fall. He pushed back the leaves and peered through his green mask's visor at the six armoured warriors on the bridge. A steady stream of clouds flowed through the chasm, occasionally obscuring Vizuna's view. From what he could see, the warriors had already taken a pounding from the monstrous six-legged Lord of Skull Spiders, who stood at the centre of the bridge. The monster's four red eyes glared at his opponents.

The six warriors were the Toa, elemental heroes from beyond time and space. Although Vizuna had heard legends of the Toa since childhood, they had arrived only recently on the island. Of the six, he had met only Lewa, Master of Jungle, who wore green armour, and was armed with swords and battle-axes that could be transformed into an X-glider that allowed Lewa to fly. But because Vizuna was so familiar with the legends, he easily recognized the other Toa.

Pohatu, Master of Stone, wore brown armour and carried a dagger and two throwing weapons that could whip up sandstorms, called stormerangs. Onua, Master of Earth, wore purple-and-black armour, and wielded an earthquake hammer and turbo shovellers. Tahu, Master of Fire, wore red armour and was equipped with two golden swords and a pair of fire blades that could be combined into a surfboard for travelling over lava. Kopaka, Master of Ice, wore white armour, and carried an ice spear and a frost shield that could be reconfigured as avalanche skis. And Gali, Master of Water, wore blue armour, and was armed with an elemental harpoon and shark fins that enabled her to swim at incredible speed.

All six Toa wore Golden Masks of Power. Ekimu the Mask Maker had crafted the masks thousands of years ago because he had predicted a day would come when the island's Protectors would need help fighting evil. Everyone on Okoto knew the legend of the Mask Makers, and how Ekimu had been forced to fight his brother, Makuta, who'd created the deadly Mask of Ultimate Power that nearly destroyed the entire island. Although Ekimu prevented total destruction, his battle with Makuta caused a cataclysm that radically transformed the island's six elemental regions into uniquely hostile environments, and left most of the island's cities in ruins. Many generations of Protectors had waited to fulfill Ekimu's prophecy. Ultimately, the duty had fallen to Vizuna and his five fellow Protectors, who had gone to the Temple of Time and summoned the six comets that delivered the Toa to Okoto.

Subsequently, each Toa arrived in a different

region on Okoto, and the Protectors had accompanied the heroes on quests to obtain the Golden Masks. Now, after many days of fighting skull spiders and other menacing creatures on their own across the island, all six Toa had finally arrived at the outskirts of the City of the Mask Makers in the Jungle Region.

But they're not united, thought Vizuna. *Not yet.*

From his treetop perch, he watched in horror as the Toa stumbled into and over one another. They appeared to be competing to determine which of them should lead the attack on the Lord of Skull Spiders. But the monster responded by spitting web fluid and flicking its legs at the Toa, easily knocking them back across the bridge. Vizuna wondered if Ekimu's prophecy had been wrong, and he shuddered at the thought.

Vizuna held his breath as the six warriors

regrouped. Behind his back, he felt his sensor tail twitch, activated by a sudden charge of elemental energy in the air. He watched the Toa surge forward in a coordinated attack against the Lord of Skull Spiders, and he felt his heart race.

Working together, the Toa blasted and slammed the six-legged monster from every angle. In less than a minute, they managed to subdue the Lord of Skull Spiders, reducing him to a heap on the bridge's central observation deck. Onua raised his earthquake hammer and brought it down hard on the bridge, breaking a large chunk of the bridge under and around the monster. The chunk fell away from the bridge and into the chasm below, carrying the monster with it.

Vizuna almost cheered out loud, but quickly remembered that he didn't want the Toa to know of his presence. Staying quiet, he watched as the Toa proceeded across the bridge to the City of the Mask Makers, which rested atop a neighbouring mountain. The city's structures included many stone spires, all of which were covered with green moss and wild vines. One such structure was the tomb of Ekimu. Even though the Toa had defeated the Lord of Skull Spiders, Vizuna imagined the city was filled with many other dangers.

After the Toa moved out of his range of vision, Vizuna descended the tree and returned to the ground. He ran quietly through the jungle, making his way towards an area where he'd planned on meeting the other Protectors. He was still running when he felt his sensor tail twitch, just a moment before he heard a branch snap behind him.

He imagined a harmless creature might have caused the noise, but he wasn't taking any chances. Without glancing back, he sprang forward, grabbed a dangling vine, and swung himself up on to a broad branch that arced high above the forest floor. Pivoting on the branch, he drew his elemental flame bow and aimed it at the jungle floor. His keen eyes peered through his mask's visor, searching for any sign of movement.

Below him, a wild plant's broad yellow leaves rustled slightly. He watched a skull spider creep out from behind the plant. The spider moved on four sharply tapered legs, and its evil eyes glowed as they flicked back and forth, eagerly searching for a victim.

Vizuna was well aware that skull spiders clamped their bodies over islanders' heads to instantly transform their victims into servants of the Lord of Skull Spiders. But now that the Toa had defeated the Lord of Skull Spiders, he wondered if skull spiders would behave differently. He silently shifted his body to aim his weapon at the spider.

He didn't see the other two skull spiders until they hit him. The impact knocked him off the branch, but the spiders clung to his green-armoured back as he fell. He knew in an instant that they must have been lurking on an upper branch, waiting for him.

Vizuna didn't need his sensor tail to tell him he would hit the ground hard if he didn't move fast. Keeping his grip on his weapon with one hand, he reached out with his other to snatch a vine. With both spiders still on his back, he clung to the vine and let his momentum carry him towards a nearby tree trunk. He rapidly shifted his legs, causing his body to turn so he was facing away from the tree. The two spiders were between him and the tree when he slammed into it, smashing his attackers.

The spiders fell away from Vizuna. They

crashed against the tree's thick roots as he released his grip on the vine. Tumbling across the ground, he rose fast, holding his flame bow in front of him as he stepped into a clearing. He scanned the surrounding trees and bushes, looking for the first evil-eyed skull spider. He was surprised when a voice called out, "Down, Vizuna!"

Vizuna recognized the voice and dropped immediately to the ground. A rapid burst of projectiles sailed over his back, tore through the thick leaves of a nearby bush, and struck the spider that had been preparing to pounce on him. The spider let out a loud screech as the projectiles sent it crashing against a tree trunk.

Vizuna rose and turned around. He saw an armoured figure wearing a black-and-purple mask step out from behind a tree. Vizuna said, "Good shooting, Korgot."

Korgot, the Protector of Earth, wore a chest-mounted rapid shooter, and carried a pair of throwing knives and an adamantine star drill that could bore through any substance. She looked at Vizuna and said, "Are you all right?"

"No harm done," Vizuna said as he brushed himself off, "at least not to me." He gestured to the fallen spiders and added, "I can't say the same for those three. They were definitely working together. The first skull spider made a noise behind me, which made me swing up to a high branch, where—"

"Where two more spiders were waiting for you," Korgot finished. "A trio of spiders tried the same tactic on me, shortly after I entered the jungle."

"Really? The spiders lured you up into a tree, too?"

"Well, they *tried*," Korgot said with a shrug. "But I just blasted them."

"Oh," said Vizuna. He felt his sensor tail twitch again. "I sense the other Protectors are approaching."

"Actually, we're already here!" came a voice from the forest. Vizuna and Korgot turned to see Narmoto, Protector of Fire, push his way through a cluster of tall ferns that grew between two trees at the edge of the clearing. Narmoto wore a red mask and armour, and carried a fire blaster and two flame swords. The white-masked Izotor, Protector of Ice – who wielded an ice blaster and a large, circular ice saw edged with sharp teeth – followed him. Next to arrive was the blue-masked Kivoda, Protector of Water, who carried an elemental torpedo blaster and wore two turbines for underwater propulsion.

The five Protectors bowed to one another in greeting. Facing Vizuna, Narmoto said, "It appears only Nilkuu is missing. I'm sure he'll be here soon, but does your sensor tail tell you how long we must wait for him?"

Vizuna shook his head. "My sensor tail can't predict *everything*."

Korgot adjusted her weapons and said, "Maybe Nilkuu got lost again? Like the last time we met at the Temple of Time?"

"I didn't get lost!" responded Nilkuu as he stumbled into the clearing. "I just took a slightly wrong turn in the mountains." Nilkuu, the Protector of Stone, wore a brown mask and carried a powerful sandstone blaster. He bowed to the other Protectors.

"It is good to see you again, my friends," said Izotor. "Many weeks have passed since we summoned the six Toa from beyond time and space to fulfil the Prophecy of Heroes."

Korgot said, "Because we're all here, I trust we all managed to greet our Toa allies after the comets delivered them to our island? And that all six Toa obtained their Golden Masks of Power before they proceeded to the City of the Mask Makers?"

The other Protectors nodded their heads in response. Narmoto said, "I'm sure we all have stories to tell of our adventures with the Toa, but now is not the time. We are on a mission!" He looked at Vizuna. "We are close to the city's gateway, yes?"

"Quite close," said Vizuna. "I've already scouted the bridge. Actually, I watched from afar as the Toa arrived. They united to fight the Lord of Skull Spiders, and—"

"Did they defeat him?" asked Kivoda.

"Yes, they did," said Vizuna.

Hearing this, the other Protectors' eyes grew wide. Although Narmoto had just discouraged everyone from telling stories, he said, "You witnessed their victory? Tell us more!"

"Well," Vizuna continued, "at first, the Toa

seemed to be fighting among themselves. But then they started working together, and their combined attack stunned the Lord of Skull Spiders, and he collapsed on the bridge. Then Onua swung his hammer down to knock a chunk out of the bridge, and that chunk carried the monster down into the chasm. Then the Toa left, moving on into the city."

"Wow," Korgot said. "I wish I'd got here sooner. I would have loved to have seen that fight!"

Izotor said, "Even with their Golden Masks and all their elemental powers, the Toa may need our help as they venture into the city in search of Ekimu the Mask Maker."

"That is why I suggested that we meet here," said Vizuna. "It may be *their* destiny to find Ekimu without us, but if the Toa require some help, it may be *our* destiny to assist them." Vizuna tilted his masked chin toward a cluster of trees at the far end of the clearing. "The bridge is that way. Follow me."

Vizuna led the other Protectors across the clearing and out of the forest. They arrived on a path that brought them into view of the monumental bridge that spanned the cloud-filled chasm to the City of the Mask Makers. Vizuna pointed to the bridge's damaged central area and said, "See the large gouge in the middle? That's where the Toa defeated the Lord of Skull Spiders, and where Onua used his hammer to send the monster falling."

Gazing at the moss-covered city in the distance beyond the bridge, Nilkuu said, "This city has always given me the creeps. It looks like an enormous graveyard."

"It wasn't always that way," Izotor said. "To our ancestors, thousands of years ago, this city was vibrant and full of life." A large cloud drifted by, briefly obscuring the city. As the cloud passed and revealed the city again, Izotor took a deep breath. "It's been a long time since I've looked upon this place. One can never forget such a sight."

"Oh!" said Nilkuu. "Speaking of never forgetting, you've just reminded me of something. Toa Pohatu has no memory of his past!"

"Really?" Korgot said. "Toa Onua doesn't remember his past, either." Glancing at her fellow Protectors, she said, "What about the rest of you? Did any Toa arrive with memories?"

"No," said the other Protectors in unison.

Vizuna said, "Perhaps that's why the Toa did not immediately work together when they met. Because they had no *memories* of working together, I guess they didn't trust one another."

"We shouldn't worry about this," said Korgot. "After all, the Toa have already battled skull spiders across the island, and obtained their

Golden Masks, right? They couldn't have done that unless they remembered one very important thing, which is that they came here to fight evil!"

"Then I guess we have nothing to worry about," Nilkuu said. "Shall we cross the bridge now to follow the Toa, or wait for them to—?"

A thunderous boom echoed across the chasm, startling the Protectors. Korgot dropped to a crouch, placed one hand on the ground, and said, "That was Onua's hammer."

"Are you certain?" said Narmoto.

"I'd know that sound anywhere. The impact came from the city. Onua must have—"

A shock wave struck the Protectors, knocking them off their feet. As they tumbled across the path, they felt the ground tremble beneath them again. Nilkuu pushed himself up from the ground, pointed to the bridge, and cried, "Look!"

Large cracks snaked through the ancient stone of the bridge's structural supports. The looming towers broke apart and fell, crashing down on to the bridge's walkway. A dark cloud of dust and debris blossomed in all directions, spewing bits of stone out over and into the chasm. The Protectors gasped as large segments of the ruined bridge appeared to rapidly sink into the river of clouds.

The Protectors moved cautiously to the edge of the cliff. A broken ledge of stone, the only remnant of the once-magnificent bridge, jutted out over the chasm.

Staring at the broken ledge, Nilkuu said, "On second thoughts, maybe we *do* have something to worry about!"

CHAPTER 2

SKULL SPIDERS ATTACK!

Still standing at the edge of the cliff, the six Protectors surveyed the wide chasm that separated them from the City of the Mask Makers. Turning to face Korgot, Narmoto said, "Are you *quite* certain Onua's hammer caused that earthquake? I thought the noise sounded like a massive explosion."

"I'm completely certain," Korgot said. "During the quest for Onua's Golden Mask in the Region of Earth, I fought alongside him long enough to recognize the sound of his hammer. But I never heard it so loud before. Obviously, he struck the ground with tremendous force . . . but why?"

"Perhaps because the Toa were under attack," said Izotor. "The Lord of Skull Spiders wasn't the only monster in the city. For all we know, they could be dealing with more powerful creatures!"

Nilkuu said, "If the Toa hoped to retreat, they definitely can't come back this way."

The clouds cleared briefly, allowing the Protectors to glimpse a pair of biomechanical cliff vultures that soared through the chasm, looking for food. As the Protector of Water, Kivoda was far more familiar with large fish than large birds, and he tried not to sound anxious as he said, "The Toa may need our help. We must find another way into the city."

Nilkuu said, "But that bridge was the *only*

way! Unless we all learn how to fly, our only option now is to climb down into the chasm and then climb up the other side. That could take days!"

"No," Vizuna said. "There is another way . . . if it still exists." He backed away from the cliff and began walking fast, heading north with the cliff to his right. "Come on. Follow me!"

The other Protectors hurried after Vizuna and quickly caught up with him. Nilkuu said, "Where are you taking us?"

"To another bridge," Vizuna said as he walked faster.

Confused, Nilkuu said, "Another bridge to the city? But . . . there isn't another one!"

"It's hardly an official bridge. Harvali, an archaeologist from a nearby village, built it. She was also an experienced mountain climber. Years ago, she discovered the existence of ancient reliefs, drawings of Okoto's Elemental

Creatures that were carved into the cliff below the City of the Mask Makers. I climbed with her so she could show them to me. She became determined to build a bridge so others could see the reliefs and study them. I tried to discourage her. I said her idea was too risky, especially with the possibility of so many dangerous creatures lurking around the cliffs. But she ignored me, and she constructed the bridge herself."

Izotor said, "But you don't know if her bridge still exists?"

"I've no idea," Vizuna said as he walked past a series of large boulders along the cliff's edge. "The last time I saw it was shortly after the local villagers informed me that Harvali was missing. That was over a year ago."

Korgot said, "You searched for her?"

"Yes. I crossed the bridge, and found marks left by skull spiders on the bridge, but no sign of Harvali. I suspect spiders attacked her. I considered destroying the bridge to prevent others from crossing it, but it occurred to me that if Harvali had survived, the bridge could be her only escape route. So I told the villagers to leave the bridge as it was, but to stay away from it."

Narmoto said, "How much further?"

"Just around that bend," Vizuna said as he pointed ahead to an area where the cliff's edge curved around the base of a stony slope. He jumped over a tree that had fallen across the path. His allies followed him over the tree, up the path, and around the bend. Clouds continued to drift through the deep chasm beside them.

Vizuna came to a stop at a rocky formation that overlooked the chasm. At the base of the formation, an arrangement of long wooden poles stuck up from the ground, angled and tied to one another to form a simple weight-bearing tower that served as the gateway for a rope bridge. Additional poles had been used to anchor the ropes and vines that secured the bridge to the cliff top. The bridge's hand and foot ropes, and also the ropes that connected them, appeared to have been skilfully knotted, but most were covered with moss, and some with jungle rot. The Protectors could see only a fragment of the bridge's length before it vanished into the clouds.

Eyeing the rotted vines, Izotor gasped. "*That's* the bridge?"

Korgot said, "Looks more like a deathtrap to me."

Vizuna hopped down and landed beside the wooden poles that formed the weight-bearing tower. He delivered two swift kicks to one pole and then kicked another. "These poles are still solid," he said as he turned his attention to the anchors. "Harvali carefully built the bridge, so it's very strong, but as you can see, some rot has set in, so we'll need to move carefully. I suggest three of us go first. I'll lead."

"Naturally," said Izotor. "As the Protector of this region, that's your privilege." He looked at the other Protectors and said, "Korgot, what say we tag along with Vizuna?"

Korgot grinned behind her mask. "By all means, let's." She turned to Nilkuu, Narmoto, and Kivoda and said, "If things go badly on the bridge, feel free to join the fight."

"Count on it!" said Narmoto.

As Izotor and Korgot followed Vizuna on to the bridge, Vizuna said, "I hope no one here is afraid of heights."

Looking down at the clouds below the bridge, Korgot said, "The Region of Earth is filled with pitfalls deeper than this."

"Heights don't scare me, either," Izotor said

as he fell into step behind Korgot, “but I’m not so crazy about impacts. I do whatever I can to avoid falling and smashing into the ground.”

Korgot responded with a hearty chuckle. Vizuna said, “All right, let’s keep it quiet. If there are any spiders in the area, we don’t want them to hear us.”

Izotor and Korgot moved carefully after Vizuna, who carefully inspected the bridge’s hand and foot ropes as he walked. He had taken only twenty steps on to the bridge when he glanced back to see that they were already so completely surrounded by clouds that he could no longer see the bridge’s gateway.

A strong gust of wind swept past the three Protectors on the bridge. They clung to the ropes until the wind passed. Vizuna had just resumed moving when his sensor tail tingled and he whispered, “Hold still.”

Izotor and Korgot froze. They heard a whooshing noise, and then they saw the two cliff vultures materialize from the dense blanket of clouds overhead. The vultures' wingspans were extremely wide, and they passed closely over the Protectors' heads before they vanished back into the clouds.

Keeping her voice low, Korgot said, "Do vultures ever attack live prey?"

"Rarely," Vizuna said, "unless they're really, really hungry."

"Then let's hope they just had a big meal," said Izotor as he proceeded after the others.

Although the three Protectors moved as quietly as possible, the bridge creaked and swayed under their weight as they moved forward. Vizuna said, "We're about halfway across. Just up ahead is where I found the marks left by skull spiders the last time I was here." He looked to his left. "Careful. The hand rope on the left is badly frayed, so lean to the right as you—"

Vizuna was interrupted by a vibration that travelled along the hand rope on the right, and then he felt the foot rope bounce. Behind him, Izotor whispered, "Is the wind making the bridge bounce?"

"I don't think so," Vizuna said. As he moved past the frayed hand rope, he reached for his elemental flame bow. Izotor and Korgot drew their own weapons as their eyes darted about behind their masks, searching for any trace of movement on the bridge in front of them or in the surrounding clouds.

Vizuna was first to see the shadowy forms of the skull spiders as they approached from the opposite direction on the bridge. He counted five spiders. Their eyes glowed and grew brighter as they advanced. Knowing that one wrong shot could split the ropes that kept the bridge suspended over the chasm, Vizuna took careful aim and released a volley of green projectiles. The blasts knocked three spiders off the hand rope and another off the foot rope, but the remaining spider sprang from the bridge, launching its body at Vizuna's head.

Vizuna swung his flame bow and struck the spider hard, knocking it aside. But just as the spider began to fall, it rapidly released a sticky strand of web to snare the bridge's foot rope. The spider swung out beneath the bridge, and its momentum caused the bridge to swing hard to one side.

Izotor braced his left foot around one of the connecting ropes as he raised his elemental ice blaster and squeezed off a shot at the swinging spider. The spider was instantly enveloped in ice. Korgot fired her rapid shooter at the spider's thread and split it. The frozen spider fell away noiselessly and vanished in the clouds.

"Ha!" Korgot said. "Skull spiders will have to try harder than that to get the best of us."

Vizuna sighed. "I wish you hadn't said that."

"Why?"

"Because my sensor tail tells me that we're about to get hit by more spiders. A *lot* more!"

The bridge jounced violently, prompting Korgot and Vizuna to brace their feet around the stringer ropes to avoid being tossed into the chasm. As Izotor checked his weapon to make sure it was fully charged, he muttered, "I don't have a sensor tail, but I have a feeling this fight is going to be ugly."

More spiders materialized from the clouds, crawling rapidly on the foot rope towards the Protectors. Vizuna's finger was poised on the trigger of his flame bow when he saw shadows out of the corner of his eye.

Looking quickly from left to right, he saw spiders abseiling on threads, swinging down from the cliffs overhead. Keeping his voice remarkably calm, he said firmly, "Korgot, left. Izotor, right."

While Vizuna kept his eyes forward, Korgot and Izotor pivoted their bodies to aim their weapons at the spiders approaching from different directions. Izotor was first to activate his weapon, launching instant-freeze projectiles at three spiders as they swung towards him. Korgot fired her rapid shooter at four spiders as they abseiled to the left of the bridge.

Vizuna squeezed the trigger of his flame bow to release green bolts of energy at the advancing skull spiders. The spiders shrieked and leaped away to avoid the bolts. Some spiders fell into the chasm, but many managed to spin threads that snared the foot rope. In a desperate effort to strike as many spiders as possible, Vizuna squeezed his trigger faster as he swung his weapon from side to side, and then down at the spiders that dangled below the bridge. But no matter how many spiders he struck, more spiders kept coming.

Two of the stringer ropes near Vizuna snapped. He realized that the spiders dangling from the foot rope were putting enormous stress on the bridge. As he blasted more spiders, he shouted to his allies, "We have to push forward!"

Korgot moved after Vizuna as they continued blasting the spiders that were coming down on either side of the bridge. Korgot shouted, "Vizuna, there's something I've wanted to ask you for a long time! Remind me if we get out of this alive!"

Vizuna called back, "*When* we get out

of this alive, I'm looking forward to that conversation!"

The bridge began bouncing even more vigorously, making it more difficult for the three Protectors to hit their targets. Vizuna assumed skull spiders had landed on the foot rope behind Korgot and Izotor, and also wondered how much longer they could hold off the monsters. He risked a quick look back and realized he was mistaken about the cause of the bouncing.

He saw Nilkuu, Narmoto, and Kivoda moving as fast as they could on the bridge, racing to help their allies. Seeing them, Vizuna felt relief, but then another stringer rope snapped and he had no doubt that the bridge would soon fall apart from the additional weight. He shouted, "Forward, Protectors!"

Spiders screeched as the six Protectors blasted their way towards the far end of the bridge. Vizuna was first to see the criss-crossed wooden poles and anchors embedded above a narrow ledge in the cliff wall below the City of the Mask Makers. As soon as he reached the poles, he turned and shot at the spiders behind him while he shouted at his allies to move on to the ledge beside him.

All six Protectors scrambled on to the ledge. Braced against the face of the cliff, they turned and blasted at the spiders on the bridge. Kivoda said, "Our weapons will run out of energy before we can stop them all!"

"Then we need to aim at a different target," Narmoto said as he set his elemental fire blaster at full power and shot at the bridge's anchors. The anchors exploded, obliterating the poles and ropes that supported the bridge's weight. The broken ropes whipped free from the anchors and the bridge fell away, carrying the spiders with it into the chasm. The spiders plummeted and vanished into the clouds.

The Protectors stood on the ledge, and were still recovering from the skirmish when Nilkuu looked at Narmoto and said, “So, when you destroyed the bridge, did you have a plan for getting us out of here?”

“Nope,” Narmoto said with a shrug. “But look on the bright side. We’re still free.”

Because of the dense cloud cover, the Protectors couldn’t see more than 6 metres in any direction. Vizuna tilted his head back to survey the cliff wall overhead, then lowered his gaze to the ledge. He said, “Climbing up would be too risky, especially if we ran into more spiders. As for this ledge, it will bring us to the ancient reliefs that I told you about. If I remember right, the ledge continues past the reliefs, so let’s see where it goes.”

Sticking close to the wall, the other

Protectors followed Vizuna along the ledge. Glancing back at Korgot, Vizuna said, "So, you had something you wanted to ask me?"

"Later," she said. "When we're on safe ground."

Landing hard on the rocks far below the broken rope bridge, the skull spiders were initially disoriented. They wandered through the chasm until they arrived before an immense pile of rubble, which was all that remained of the monumental bridge to the City of the Mask Makers. Wending their way over and around the rubble, they eventually found the defeated Lord of Skull Spiders.

The sight of their fallen master filled the spiders with rage. The spiders chittered to one another. Although their intelligence was almost as limited as their ability to communicate, they agreed to bring their master to a safe place to help him heal and recover. They vowed to honour him by continuing to capture and enslave the islanders of Okoto.

They were also determined to hunt down the Toa and the Protectors, and they were willing to do whatever was necessary to accomplish their goals.

Still dazed from their fall, but eager to resume their reign of terror over the island, the spiders worked fast, spinning protective webs around their master. Once their master was secured, one group of spiders began hauling him towards the base of a cliff, where another group of spiders was already busily spinning long threads that travelled up and down the cliff's face. Although clouds obscured the view overhead, the spiders knew that the cliff led all the way up to the City of the Mask Makers.

Working together, and fuelled by thoughts of revenge, the skull spiders began hauling their unconscious master up the cliff.

CHAPTER 3

THE MYSTERIOUS CAVE

Vizuna led the Protectors along the ledge, which began to curve around the cliff wall. They moved slowly, facing the wall as they shifted their hands from side to side, their fingers seizing upon any rocky outgrowth or small crack in the surface that could serve as a hand hold. No one looked down, because there was nothing to see but clouds.

The ledge widened slightly, and Vizuna realized they were approaching the reliefs that the archaeologist Harvali had shown him years earlier. He said, "We're coming up to the ancient carvings now."

And then the Protectors saw the reliefs. The carved pictograms displayed six different creatures configured within a diamond-shaped pattern – a symbolic map of Okoto. Each creature represented an Elemental Creature of the island and was a dragon-like version of an existing animal. Melum, the Creature of Ice, seemed like a hybrid of an ape and a rhinoceros. Akida, the Creature of Water, resembled a shark. Uxar, the Creature of Jungle, looked like a dragonfly. Ikir, the Creature of Fire, was some sort of bird of prey. Terak, the Creature of Earth, appeared as an apelike lizard. And Ketar, the Creature of Stone, was a scorpion. Additional pictograms, symbols, and possible letterforms radiated around the ancient map.

"Fascinating!" said Izotor. "This map appears to indicate the location of the Temple of Time, and also the regions of the Elemental Creatures. But most of the letters baffle me."

"I've never seen writing like that, either," Korgot said. "And the carvings don't show the Mask Makers or their city."

Nilkuu stared hard at the map. "Perhaps these reliefs were made long before the Mask Makers were born?"

"Possibly," said Vizuna. "That's what Harvali believed, and what she hoped to prove."

"Enough sightseeing," said Kivoda. "If we're going to find the Toa, let's move!"

Leaving the reliefs behind, Vizuna resumed his steady shuffle, leading the others along the ledge. As he began to edge around another curve, Nilkuu said, "Vizuna, can you see anything up ahead?"

"No," Vizuna replied. "The clouds are too thick, and . . . Oh! I see something dark."

"What is it?"

Vizuna moved closer to the dark area. "It looks like the mouth of a cave. I can't see how deep it is, but I think it's large enough for us to rest for a few—"

A strong gust of wind struck the Protectors, prompting them to flatten their bodies against the cliff. The wind tugged at the turbines mounted to Kivoda's back, causing him to lose his balance. He gasped as he began to fall away from the ledge, but then he felt a tight pressure against his left wrist and he stopped short.

"Got you!" said Izotor, who clutched at Kivoda's wrist with one hand while clinging to the cliff's face with the other. Izotor was just starting to pull Kivoda back towards the wall when the two vultures appeared from out of the clouds.

The first vulture swooped so close to Kivoda that the large bird's wing knocked him away from the ledge. Kivoda fell back again, this time taking Izotor with him. Korgot jumped after both of them and managed to hook her feet over the edge of the cliff while she reached out and grabbed Izotor's left leg. Izotor held tight to Kivoda, and they both dangled below Korgot's tight grip.

Narmoto, Vizuna and Nilkuu had already drawn their weapons as the second vulture dived down from above, its talons poised to tear Korgot and the others off the ledge. Narmoto and Vizuna aimed for the vulture's right wing while Nilkuu fired his sandstone blaster straight at the vulture's head. The vulture shrieked as the Protectors' combined firepower knocked it off course, causing it to swerve past Korgot and slam into the cliff's face below. The vulture bounced off the rock and disappeared into the clouds.

Vizuna saw one of Korgot's feet begin to

slip over the cliff's edge. Keeping his flame bow aimed at the sky, he crouched down and used his free hand to grab Korgot's foot. The first vulture swooped back and Vizuna launched a round of projectiles that whizzed past the approaching bird. Nilkuu and Narmoto saw the vulture, too, and fired at it, catching it in the chest. The vulture let out a loud squawk as it descended fast in pursuit of its falling partner, and then both vultures were lost from sight.

Nilkuu and Narmoto moved fast to help Vizuna haul Korgot, Izotor, and Kivoda back on to the ledge. As soon as Kivoda caught his breath, he said, "Next time we go mountain climbing, remind me to leave my turbines at home."

"Come on," Vizuna said. "Let's get going before those vultures come back."

Vizuna was about to enter the cave when

Korgot stopped him and said, "Hold it right there. Caves are my specialty, and I have excellent vision in darkness. Allow me." Korgot adjusted her chest-mounted rapid shooter as she moved past Vizuna to enter the cave first. The others followed.

The cave's rocky ceiling was just high enough that none of the Protectors had to duck. "Watch your step," Korgot said. "Some old spider-webs are stretched across the ground. I don't think any spiders have been in here for a while, but the webs are still sticky."

Vizuna said, "My sensor tail doesn't detect any life-forms in here except for us."

"Keep your eyes open for spiders anyway," said Narmoto. "They have a nasty habit of appearing when we least expect them."

Korgot chuckled. "If I see any spiders, you'll know, because I'll be the first one to open fire on them." She moved deeper into the cave until she came to a stop and said, "Narmoto, can you shine a light over here?"

Narmoto ignited one of his flame swords and the cave's walls were suddenly illuminated by the blade's warm yellow light. He moved closer to Korgot, who pointed at a large pile of rocks that sloped down and away from one wall. Korgot said, "I feel a slight breeze. Beyond these rocks, there's another chamber."

Nilkuu leaned forward to examine the rocks and said, "Looks like a cave-in sealed off the passage."

"Looks like it," Korgot said, "but it's not a cave-in. See how all the larger stones are at the bottom of the pile? It's all too neatly done. Someone *put* those rocks there, and placed the smaller rocks on top of the heavier ones."

"But why?" said Kivoda. "To keep spiders out?"

"Possibly," Korgot said. "Keep in mind we're

below the City of the Mask Makers. For all we know, these rocks may be blocking a passage that leads up to the city. There's only one way to find out. We're going through."

Korgot reached for her adamantine star drill while the other Protectors stood back, giving her room to work. She placed the drill's tip against the wall of solid rock to the left of the rubble-filled passageway and then powered up the device. The noise was so loud that Nilkuu winced behind his mask. Korgot pushed the drill forward and instantly transformed the slab of stone before her into a large, dusty hole. She made a slight adjustment to the drill to expand the hole, making it large enough for each Protector to pass through without damaging their armour or weapons.

Korgot stepped through the hole first and moved past several large boulders. Narmoto, who held his ignited flame sword in front of him so the others could see where they were going, followed her. They entered a chamber that was much larger than the cave's entrance, so large that Narmoto instinctively drew his second sword to illuminate a wider area around him.

Looking back at the fresh hole in the wall, Korgot said, "We'd better seal this so spiders won't get in. Nilkuu, give me a hand here."

Nilkuu helped Korgot shift three boulders to block the hole. When they were done, Korgot gazed into the depths of the cave and said, "The breeze is coming from this way." She gestured for the others to follow her.

They walked past a series of large stalactites, like icicles of rock, that had formed by water dripping from the ceiling over the course of many centuries. Behind Korgot, Nilkuu glanced at one stalactite and said,

"Hey, take a look at this!"

The others stopped and turned to look at Nilkuu's discovery. He faced a wide column of rock – a stalagmite – that extended up to connect with a stalactite hanging from the ceiling. The natural column appeared to be almost completely covered with carved reliefs.

"Wow," said Korgot. "I can't believe I walked right past this."

The Protectors immediately recognized various symbols and figures that represented the ancient Protectors. "See here," Vizuna said as he pointed to a pair of pictograms. "These represent Ekimu and Makuta. I'm guessing these carvings aren't as old as the ones on the cliff wall. I can read most of the letters, too."

Moving slowly around the column, Izotor said, "This really is amazing. These images illustrate the history of the Prophecy of Heroes. Here's Ekimu when he sees the six Elemental

Creatures during the Festival of Masks, and he considers their appearance an omen." Izotor pointed to the next sequence of pictograms and said, "And here, Ekimu and the Protectors – our ancestors – go to the Temple of Time, and Ekimu uses the Mask of Time to see into the future. That's how he learned about the cataclysm that would change Okoto's geography, and also how he learned that six comets would eventually deliver the Toa to our island."

Narmoto leaned in beside Izotor and said, "And look, there's Ekimu crafting the Masks of Power to prepare for the day when the Toa would arrive. And this part illustrates the cataclysm!"

Kivoda said, "Must I remind you all again that we're on a mission? Come now, let's not dawdle any longer."

Nilkuu leaned closer to the column and

said, "Wait, Kivoda. According to these images, long after the cataclysm, the Toa find Ekimu's body in the City of the Mask Makers, and Ekimu returns to life. Then the Protectors – that means us – arrive in the city, and we bow before Ekimu. You know what that means?"

"That we're wasting our time here?" said Kivoda.

"No! It means that it's our *destiny* to reach the city! To meet Ekimu, and reunite with the Toa! We have nothing to worry about!"

Korgot groaned. "Nilkuu, remember what happened the last time you said we had nothing to worry about? The bridge to the city collapsed."

"Enough!" said Kivoda with obvious impatience. "Let's proceed." He started walking away from the column, stepping on to a long slab of stone that lay across the cave's floor and led towards another passage. Narmoto, holding his flame swords out to light the way, walked behind Kivoda while the others followed.

"Careful," Kivoda said. "This rock is a bit slippery." He had taken less than a dozen steps across the long slab before it tilted suddenly under his feet, transforming the slab into a long ramp that simultaneously lowered Kivoda while it lifted the Protectors behind him. All six Protectors slid and tumbled down the ramp and into a deep, smooth-walled hole.

Falling in front of Kivoda, Narmoto clung to his flame swords and held them away from his body, taking care not to accidentally jab his allies. The hole curved sharply and Kivoda tried to brace his feet to stop falling, but the walls were too slick. From behind, he heard Korgot shout, "We're in a lava tube!"

The hole widened and Narmoto was first to launch out into the air and almost total darkness, but his bright swords enabled him to see that the hole emptied into a wide pit that was filled with sharp-tipped stalagmites. Still falling, he somersaulted through the air while sweeping his swords from front to back, cutting down the nearest stalagmites and then landing between them. The shattered stalagmites fell away to the sides of the pit just as the other five Protectors crashed down around Narmoto.

"What a ride!" said Korgot as she got up and brushed herself off. "We're fortunate that we fell into an ancient lava tube instead of an active one."

"Yeah, lucky us," Vizuna groaned as he sat up and adjusted his mask.

Narmoto said, "Everyone all right?"

"I think so," said Nilkuu. "But from now on, I think I'll stop saying 'We have nothing to worry about.'"

Kivoda said, "And I'll take better care to

watch my step. I'm sorry I got us into this mess."

"It's not your fault," said Izotor. "Accidents happen."

Korgot said, "Izotor's right, Kivoda, it's not your fault. But I don't think we fell down that hole entirely by accident. I'm guessing someone shifted and positioned that rock over the lava tube as a trap to capture trespassers."

Nilkuu said, "Maybe it was the same someone who made the blocked passage look like a cave-in?"

"Could be," said Korgot. She looked at the broken stalagmites and walls of the pit, then lifted her gaze to the hole in the ceiling. "Going back the way we came would take too long. Unless we can find a passage out of here, I'll use my drill to create a new—"

Hearing a shuffling noise from the far side

of the pit, Korgot went silent. The other Protectors heard the noise, too. Korgot signalled Narmoto to extinguish the light from his swords. The swords went dark, but Narmoto continued holding them while his allies quietly readied their own weapons and listened.

Peering across the pit, Korgot saw a shadowy form move behind a wide stalagmite. A few seconds later, a single figure peeked out from behind the stalagmite. Despite the darkness, Korgot could clearly see that the figure wore a green mask and was holding a spear. "Well, well, well," she said to her allies. "I believe we've located the missing archaeologist!"

"Hold your fire," Vizuna said to the other Protectors. Rising from the pit, he called out, "Harvali, is that you? It is me, Vizuna of the Jungle Region."

From the darkness, a female islander responded in a raspy voice, "Vizuna?"

Vizuna nudged Narmoto and said, "Please ignite your swords again."

Narmoto's swords blazed to life, filling the pit with light. The Protectors watched as the green-masked islander emerged from behind the stalagmite and walked towards them.

Harvali stared at the six Protectors as if she could hardly believe her eyes. She bowed to Vizuna, who bowed in return. She said, "I . . . I never thought you'd find me." She had to clear her throat before she continued. "I can't remember the last time I talked out loud. I'm sorry I didn't heed your warnings about the risks of studying the reliefs." She cleared her throat again. "I'm also sorry you fell into my trap. I made it to stop skull spiders." She looked at all the Protectors. "All of you came searching for me?"

"Not exactly," Vizuna said. "After your neighbours reported you missing, I looked for you, but failed to find more than spider tracks on your bridge. I assumed that the spiders had claimed you. I regret I didn't search longer. But another mission brought me and my fellow Protectors here, and . . . and I am glad and relieved to see you."

"I wish I could say the same," Harvali said. "I'm afraid you and all the Protectors might now be trapped in here. For ever!"

CHAPTER 4

AN UNEXPECTED ALLY

Surprised by Harvali's statement, Vizuna glanced back at his fellow Protectors, then returned his attention to Harvali and said, "What makes you think we'll never get out of this cavern?"

A loud hiss filled the air. Harvali cringed as she tightened her grip on her spear. She whispered, "We'll talk later. We must move fast to the next chamber before that biomechanical snake gets here."

"Snake?" said Izotor. "How big is it?"

"Very big." Motioning for the Protectors to follow her, Harvali turned and sprinted towards a narrow gap between two boulders that extended from the cave's floor to its ceiling. As she led Vizuna, Korgot, Narmoto, Kivoda and Izotor through the gap, she said, "The snake can't fit through here."

Running behind the group, Nilkuu had nearly reached the gap when something struck the side of his foot, sending him sprawling. He rolled across the rocky ground and came up standing. Drawing his sandstone blaster, he spun fast to face a massive biomechanical snake covered with armoured scales. As the snake rose up before him, he could see that the ventral scales covering its belly were also heavily armoured. Although he didn't have a clear view of the snake's head, he could see that its eyes were glowing red. Its tail moved from side to side.

Nilkuu realized the snake must have used its tail to trip him. Despite the darkness, he guessed the snake was at least eight times longer than his own height. With a loud hiss, the snake moved closer to him, and he saw that a large skull spider covered its upper head and eyes.

Izotor and Kivoda noticed that Nilkuu had fallen behind, so they turned around in the nearby passage and looked back to see that their ally was in trouble. Izotor shouted, "Nilkuu!"

Nilkuu fired his sandstone blaster at the skull spider. Blistering sand slammed into the spider, knocking it off the snake's head. The spider screeched as the blast carried its body straight into the ceiling before gravity delivered it to the ground.

The snake looked at Nilkuu with a dazed expression, then shook its head back and forth, as if it were trying to shake off an invisible enemy. Then the snake spotted the motionless spider. The snake lifted its tail and brought the tail down hard, thwacking the spider with such force that it bounced across the cave.

Shifting its own long body again, the snake moved toward Nilkuu. He took an instinctive step backward, but then the snake stuck out its tongue and licked the side of Nilkuu's mask. Nilkuu said, "Does that mean we're friends now?" The snake licked his mask again and bobbed its head up and down, happily.

Nilkuu chuckled. Looking away from the snake, he saw Izotor and Kivoda watching him. "What do you know?" he said. "This snake is playful!"

"Well, stop playing around and get in here!" said Izotor.

Nilkuu patted the side of the snake's head. Leaving the snake, he followed his allies into the next chamber. The chamber was smaller than the previous one, but was illuminated by shiny stones. Narmoto had dimmed his flame swords, but Nilkuu could see that the chamber's walls, ceiling, and even parts of the stone floor were covered with ancient reliefs. Vizuna and Korgot stood near Harvali, who sat huddled on a wide rock beside a bubbling pool of water. Small plants with dark blue and purple leaves surrounded the pool.

Facing Harvali, Nilkuu aimed a thumb at the chamber's passageway and said, "Don't worry about the snake. I knocked the spider off of its head. The snake is friendly now."

"Thank goodness!" said Harvali. "I tried using my spear to get rid of that spider, but I could never get close enough." She gestured to the reliefs on the walls. "As you can see, there's much to study down here." She looked at the pool and plants. "I was lucky to find water and edible plants soon after I became trapped, but . . . we'll have to grow more plants if we're all going to survive in here."

Vizuna said, "Again, I ask: why are you so convinced that we'll never escape?"

"Because I've been living underground for over a year, and I've explored every passage. There are only two routes in and out, but they're both impassable. You must have entered the same way I did, by way of the ledge." Behind her mask, Harvali's eyes went wide with concern. "I hope you sealed off the passage to prevent spiders from getting in!"

"It's sealed," Korgot said. "However, that route isn't much of an option any more, because your rope bridge is gone."

"What?"

"I blasted it to stop scores of spiders from attacking us," Narmoto admitted.

Harvali shook her head. "Then we're definitely permanently trapped!"

"Relax," Korgot said. "I have a friend here who can help us create another way out." She held up her star drill for Harvali to see. "This drill can bore through anything!"

"But drilling takes time," Vizuna said, "and we're in a bit of a hurry. Harvali, allow me to bring you up to speed. The Prophecy of Heroes has come to pass. Weeks ago, the Toa arrived on Okoto. Earlier today, they defeated the Lord of Skull Spiders and entered the City of the Mask Makers. Unfortunately, the city's main bridge was destroyed. Because the Toa may be in need of help, my fellow Protectors and I sought a different route into the city. Which brought us here. So, please, tell us about the other route you mentioned."

Harvali's eyes grew even wider behind her mask. "The Toa are really here?" She grasped the edges of her mask in astonishment and shook her head again. "All this information is a lot to absorb. And I don't understand . . . I thought the Lord of Skull Spiders controlled all the skull spiders. But if the Toa defeated him, why was the giant snake still under the spider's control?"

"Because evil forces are still at large," said Vizuna, "and the spiders are a part of that evil."

"The only other route out of the caverns," Harvali said, "is through the Lord of Skull Spiders' lair. I never dared attempt to enter that chamber before, but if you're certain he's no longer a threat—?"

"With my own eyes," Vizuna interjected, "I saw the Toa defeat the Lord of Skull Spiders, and saw his body plunge into the chasm that surrounds the city."

"Very well," said Harvali as she stood up. "I shall guide you to the Lord of Skull Spiders' lair, and up to the city." She looked around at the reliefs. "If we do survive, I vow to return to this place and make sure it's preserved, along with the reliefs in the caves." She led the Protectors out of the chamber.

They found the large snake waiting outside. Seeing Nilkuu, the snake bobbed its head again.

Harvali looked at the snake warily, then pointed beyond the pit filled with stalagmites to a dark area. She said, "We'll go through a series of tunnels that way. I hope you're ready for a long walk!"

The snake lowered its head beside Nilkuu. Nilkuu was about to give the snake a pat when the creature tucked its head below Nilkuu's arm and lifted him off his feet. Nilkuu said, "Hey!"

The snake twisted its head and lowered Nilkuu so he straddled the snake's back. The snake slithered forward, then looked at the other Protectors and Harvali. Nilkuu said, "I think my new friend is offering us a ride."

Harvali said, "The snake *can* move very fast through the tunnels, but are you sure it's safe to ride?"

"Only one way to find out," Korgot said. She hopped up on to the snake's back behind Nilkuu. The snake nodded at her. "What are the rest of you waiting for? Climb on!"

"I think I'm going to regret this," Harvali muttered as she climbed up on to the snake. The remaining Protectors hopped on to the snake's back and locked their fingers beneath the creature's scales.

The snake took off with surprising speed. The snake's riders tightened their grips on its scales as their mount swerved around each stalagmite in its path, heading into a tunnel that sloped upward. Because the snake was travelling swiftly through almost total darkness, Korgot assumed its night vision was as good as her own. But as the snake rounded a corner in the tunnel, Korgot looked ahead and shouted, "Everyone duck! Low stalactites up ahead!"

All seven riders hunkered down close against the snake's back. As the snake rounded another corner, Korgot lifted her head and said, "All clear, but everyone should stay low."

Nilkuu said, "A little light would help. Narmoto?"

Narmoto clung tight to the snake with one hand as he drew a flame sword and ignited it, allowing the riders to see the cave's walls and ceiling flowing past them. Sounding slightly queasy, Harvali said, "I think I felt safer when I *couldn't* see how fast we were moving."

Looking ahead, Nilkuu said, "There's a fork in the tunnel. Harvali, which way do we go?"

"To the left!" Harvali gasped.

Nilkuu shifted his weight to the left and was very surprised when the snake swerved to the right. As the snake travelled into the wrong tunnel, Nilkuu said, "Oops. Maybe I should have practised steering before we got moving."

"There's a lava tube on the left!" Harvali shouted. "Take it or we'll plunge into an underground chasm!"

Nilkuu saw the opening of the lava tube and shifted his weight to the right. The snake swerved into the lava tube. Nilkuu said, "I think I'm getting the hang of this!"

The snake hurtled up through the lava tube but slowed down as it neared the tube's exit, a wide hole that emptied into a wide cave. Slithering into the cave, the snake came to a stop alongside a rock wall, then twisted its head back to look at Nilkuu. Nilkuu said, "Why'd you stop? Are you tired?"

Harvali eased herself down to the ground. "I'm guessing the snake senses we're close to the Lord of Skull Spiders' lair, and doesn't want to go farther. Come on. We'll proceed on foot."

The Protectors climbed off the snake. Nilkuu gave the snake one more pat and said, "Thanks for the ride, pal. If you ever get tired of these caves, you should visit me in the Region of Stone."

Leaving the snake, Harvali led the Protectors up a series of staggered boulders. When they reached the top, they stood before the mouth of another tunnel. A strange scraping noise echoed down the length of the tunnel. Turning to face Vizuna, Harvali whispered, "You're absolutely certain you saw the Lord of Skull Spiders plunge into the chasm?"

"Yes," Vizuna said, "but my sensor tail is telling me there's danger ahead." He looked at his fellow Protectors. "We should stick together. Korgot, you'll lead and serve as lookout. The rest of us will stay close, and watch one another's backs." Returning his attention to Harvali, he continued, "I hope you still want to come with us, because even though we don't know what's ahead, I'm not about to leave you here alone."

"Oh, I'm coming with you, all right," said Harvali as she adjusted her grip on her spear.

Walking as quietly as possible, they entered the dark tunnel. They hadn't walked far when they heard a dripping noise. Korgot whispered, "I see water dripping from the ceiling. And a puddle on the ground up ahead. But just keep walking. No sign of any spiders."

Keeping his voice low, Kivoda said, "Where's that water coming from?"

Harvali replied, "Underground reservoirs that collect rainwater below the city. They've been crumbling and falling apart for centuries."

The scraping noise echoed through the tunnel again, only slightly louder. Izotor whispered, "We must be getting closer to whatever's making that sound."

The tunnel floor began to incline. The Protectors and Harvali stealthily plodded on gravelly stones through the darkness. Korgot guided them around a bend in the tunnel, and they all saw a dim light in the distance. They proceeded towards the light, which appeared to glow brighter as they advanced, until they were close enough to see they were approaching the end of the tunnel, and that the light emanated from beyond.

They heard the scraping noise again, only it sounded longer and louder. Staying close to the tunnel's shadowy walls, they crept up to the tunnel's exit. Korgot was first to peek outside. She quickly drew her head back to the shadows, turned to face her allies, and said, "I hope you're all feeling braver than usual right now."

“Why?” said Narmoto.

“Because that scraping noise is the sound of hundreds of skull spiders hauling their master into the cave just outside this tunnel.”

“What?” said Izotor. He peeked into the cave, then ducked back into the tunnel and said, “Korgot, I don’t mean to quibble, but I believe it would be more accurate to say ‘over a thousand skull spiders’.”

Vizuna and Harvali each stole a glance into the cave. They saw the Lord of Skull Spiders wrapped in silk spun by the skull spiders. The spiders were tugging at the threads to draw their master deeper into the cave, away from the cave’s mouth, which opened on to the chasm that surrounded the City of the Mask Makers. They also saw fine streams of water trickling down from the cave’s ceiling. Harvali pointed to the dark entrance of a passage on the far side of the cave, and whispered, “That’s the way back up to the city."

They ducked back into the tunnel. Vizuna said, "The Lord of Skull Spiders appears to be unconscious."

Harvali said, "But we'll never make it to the next passage, not with thousands of skull spiders in the way!"

"Not 'thousands,'" Izotor corrected, "but definitely over a thousand."

"What's the difference?" Harvali said. "We're beyond greatly outnumbered!"

Narmoto peeked into the cave. "I've never seen so many spiders in one place before. They must have come from all over the Jungle Region to . . . to mobilize! That must be the reason. They're grouping here because they're preparing for war!"

Vizuna said, "They're probably seeking revenge. They'll go after the Toa and also us. We can't let them do that, especially if the Toa are already busy dealing with other monsters in the city."

Harvali said, "What can *we* do? There are only seven of us!"

Turning to face Harvali, Nilkuu said, "When you studied the reliefs, didn't you see the bit that showed the Protectors meeting Ekimu after the Toa arrive?"

Harvali gave Nilkuu a blank stare. "What does that have to do with anything?"

"Well," said Nilkuu, "we, the Protectors, have yet to meet Ekimu, but we *will*, because the reliefs said so. It's in our *future*. So relax. We'll all live. There's nothing to worry about!"

Korgot punched Nilkuu in the arm. "You told us that you'd stop saying that!"

"Oops," said Nilkuu. "I forgot."

Harvali returned her gaze to Vizuna. "We can't possibly sneak past that many spiders."

"Which is why we're not going to sneak past

them," said Vizuna. "Here's the plan."

Vizuna told the group his plan. When he was finished, Kivoda said, "Yeah, that should do the trick."

Harvali shook her head and said, "You're all bonkers."

The Protectors ran out of the tunnel and into the cave. All the skull spiders stopped what they were doing and turned their evil gazes toward the Protectors. And then the Protectors opened fire.

CHAPTER 5

ESCAPE FROM THE SPIDERS' LAIR

Seeing the Protectors

invade their master's lair, over a thousand skull spiders screeched angrily. The spiders that had been hauling the unconscious Lord of Skull Spiders deeper into the cave released their threads, and joined the vicious mob that skittered quickly towards the entrance to the tunnel where the Protectors stood firing their weapons.

But then the spiders noticed that the Protectors weren't shooting directly at them, but were instead shooting over their heads. The spiders collectively paused, glanced upward, and saw that the Protectors were concentrating their firepower on a long, leaking crack in the cave's ceiling.

The crack was directly above the Lord of Skull Spiders' body.

The Protectors continued to bombard the ceiling. The crack began to expand, and then water exploded out from the centre of the crack, bringing large, wet chunks of broken stone crashing down upon the Lord of Skull Spiders. The spiders closest to their master screeched as they tried to dodge the falling rubble. Not all of them succeeded.

The crack in the cave's ceiling expanded even more, and then it fractured loudly. Water sprayed out and cascaded across the cave, and larger segments of the ceiling broke away. The spiders didn't know which way to run.

Some skittered back to the threads that secured their master, and tried to pull him away from the falling rubble. Others simply tried to dodge the rocks. Hundreds of spiders stumbled and tripped over one another in their haste to reach safety.

The remaining spiders narrowed their gazes on the Protectors, and advanced towards them. Behind the Protectors, standing just outside the tunnel, Harvali shouted, "Look out! A group of spiders is coming straight for you!"

The Protectors knew exactly what to do. Nilkuu lowered his sandstone blaster and fired at the approaching spiders, knocking the nearest spiders off their spindly legs, and causing them to trip the spiders directly behind them. Kivoda launched a wide spray of water from his torpedo blaster, thoroughly drenching the wretched creatures, before Izotor used his ice blaster to freeze the soaked spiders. The

Protectors' teamwork resulted in a broad pile of frozen spiders that served as a wall between them and the still-active spiders.

But a second wave of spiders began furiously scrambling over their frozen comrades. To avoid slipping on the icy figures, the spiders dug their sharp-tipped legs into the ice as they surged toward the Protectors.

Nilkuu, Kivoda and Izotor had already raised their weapons and resumed blasting at the cave's ceiling as the second wave of spiders approached. Vizuna increased power to his elemental flame bow and released a wide burst of bright green projectiles at the spiders, stunning many of them while temporarily blinding the others. Narmoto followed with his elemental fire blaster, spraying the frozen spiders with a blast of heat that sent them reeling backwards. As for the spiders that had endured the attack, they were unprepared for when Korgot opened fire with her rapid shooter, blasting several stalactites that dangled overhead. The stalactites fell like massive projectiles from the ceiling and landed on the spiders.

The Protectors and Harvali took a step back as the fallen stalactites threw up clouds of dust. The air in the cave had also become thick with rising steam as water continued to stream down from the ruined ceiling. Although the Protectors had subdued many skull spiders, some still chittered and screeched to one another throughout the cave.

Korgot felt a tremor in the ground. Thudding and crunching noises followed, Korgot gazed through the dusty haze and focused on the layers of rocks and dirt that covered the Lord of Skull Spiders.

The rocks and dirt were shifting and sliding away from the monster's body.

"The Lord of Skull Spiders is waking up!" Korgot said. Her allies looked at the monster. Although the Lord of Skull Spiders was still bound by the strong threads that his minions had spun, his evil red eyes glowed brightly, and he was obviously straining against the threads.

"We have to get past the Lord of Skull Spiders to reach the passage," said Izotor.

"Uh-oh," said Narmoto. "More spiders are coming in through the cave's mouth!"

"We can't just stand here," Harvali said. "Should we retreat?"

Before any of the Protectors could answer, they heard a loud hiss from behind. Glancing back, they saw the giant snake slither out from the tunnel that had brought them to the Lord of Skull Spiders' lair. Surprised, Nilkuu said, "Well, I didn't expect to see you again so soon!"

A loud snap came from across the cave.

The Protectors saw that one of the Lord of Skull Spiders' legs had just broken through several thick strands of spider thread. The monster's leg flexed and twitched, then started to tug at the other strands that bound his body.

The giant snake moved up next to Nilkuu and licked the side of his mask. Nilkuu said, "I think the snake wants to get out of here just as much as we do." He pointed to the passage on the other side of the cave as he faced the snake and said, "If I keep the spiders off you, can you get all of us over there?"

The snake's head bobbed up and down. Nilkuu hopped up on to the snake's back and said, "Climb on, everyone!"

The other Protectors and Harvali climbed quickly on to the snake and grabbed hold of its scales. Nilkuu braced his sandstone blaster so it extended over the top of the snake's head, then said, "Let's go!"

Moving even faster than it had earlier, the snake sped forward, ploughing over and through the wall of frozen spiders. The clustered spiders saw the snake coming but weren't fast enough to assume an attack formation or get out of the way. The snake's armoured belly smashed into the spiders, knocking them aside.

Another loud snapping noise came from the Lord of Skull Spiders as he managed to release two more legs from the binding web. The monster extended his legs to kick at the ground and upended his body so he could more easily start tearing at the threads that bound his remaining legs.

As the snake hurtled across the cave, Kivoda and Narmoto blasted at the ceiling overhead, shattering it to bring down more rocks and water onto the surrounding spiders. Nilkuu made sure the snake stayed on course, heading for the passage. But as the snake sped past the Lord of Skull Spiders, the Protectors heard the evil monster roar as his legs broke free from the threads. The monster moved fast, skittering after the snake with alarming speed.

A group of about thirty spiders near the passage realized the snake was coming straight toward them. They scurried in front of the passage, climbed on top of one another, and rapidly arranged themselves into a pyramid formation to block the snake's path. Nilkuu realized the spiders were poised to give at least one of them a good chance of latching on to the snake's head when it came into contact with them. They were also poised to latch on to the snake's riders.

Nilkuu wasn't going to let that happen. He fired his blaster five times in quick succession. The spiders shrieked as the blasts struck them, causing them to release one another and making their pyramid fall apart. The rattled spiders shrieked again as the snake, still carrying its seven riders, sped into the passage.

The Lord of Skull Spiders was right behind the snake and about to snare its tail when the cave's entire ceiling collapsed with a thunderous crash. Kivoda and Narmoto glanced back just in time to see the monster and his remaining minions buried by the rubble. Dust and dirt sprayed after the fleeing heroes, but the snake managed to carry its riders into the passage unharmed.

"That was too close!" said Narmoto.

The snake sped forward. The passage led directly to a series of broad stone steps in a circular stairwell. With its seven riders still clinging to its back, the snake travelled swiftly up the stairwell, its armoured belly clacking against the stones as it climbed higher and higher. The top of the stairwell ended at an open circular doorway. The snake shot through the doorway and came to a skidding stop outdoors, in a field that was filled with weeds and high grass.

"We made it!" Nilkuu said, jumping down from the snake's back. As the other Protectors climbed down to the ground, he patted the snake's head and said, "Thanks again, pal!"

"Daylight!" said Harvali, squinting as she joined the Protectors. "It's been so long since I've seen it, so very long since I've breathed fresh air."

The Protectors looked around, and saw that the grassy field was enclosed by a high stone wall. Dozens of stone obelisks and statues loomed throughout the field, and most of the monuments were choked with thick vines. Narmoto said, "Check out all the tombstones."

Nilkuu said, "That explains why this place gives me the creeps!"

"I believe we're in one of the older graveyards," Harvali said, "along the city's outskirts. I've never been here before, but I did study ancient maps of the city." As she pushed through the high grass to take a closer look at a monument, she felt something brush against her left foot. She was still moving towards the monument when she felt cold, bony fingers grab her ankle.

Harvali screamed. Korgot leaped beside Harvali and brought her own foot down hard, stomping on the skeletal arm that had seized her. The bony fingers popped open, releasing their grip.

Korgot picked up the skeletal arm and inspected it carefully. "No doubt about it. This came from a skull warrior." She tossed the arm aside, letting it crash against the base of a monument. Facing Harvali, she said, "We'd best watch our step. There may be more underfoot."

A wide area of ground erupted beside the giant snake, shoving it backwards against a long wall, and then dozens of skull warriors pushed their way up through the soil and dirt. Most of the skeletal creatures carried swords and shields, but some were armed with bows and arrows. Using their glowing red eyes to select their targets, the archers drew their bows and released their arrows at the Protectors.

"Take cover!" Narmoto shouted.

Korgot grabbed Harvali and dived behind a monument a split second before deadly arrows whizzed over the grass where they'd just been standing. Korgot darted around the monument and opened fire with her rapid shooter, mowing down the nearest archers.

Several skull warriors jumped on top of the giant snake, which had become pinned between the upended ground and the wall.

The warriors swung their swords down on the snake's scales hard enough to make the snake release a pained hiss. Nilkuu and Izotor blasted at the snake's attackers, smashing the skull warriors against the wall. Their brittle bones broke upon impact, just as the snake wrenched itself from the ground.

Three arrows whizzed past Vizuna. The Protector of Jungle ducked behind a tree and came up fast, bracing his flame bow against a branch before releasing a barrage of projectiles at the remaining archers. The projectiles struck the archers and snapped their bones, causing them to collapse. Vizuna turned his attention to his allies, and saw three skull warriors sneaking up behind the Protector of Water. He shouted, "Kivoda, behind you!"

Kivoda instinctively ducked and tumbled sideways, just as the three skull warriors swung their swords. The blades narrowly missed

Kivoda as he rolled across the grass. When he came to a stop, all three warriors were within the sights of his torpedo blaster. The watery blast knocked the skeletons off their leg bones, and their other bones clattered against one another before they hit the ground and separated into hundreds of pieces.

Two more sword-bearing skull warriors moved quickly towards Narmoto. The Protector of Fire drew his flame swords as he leaped over both warriors. He landed behind them, and as they spun around to confront him, both fell upon his swords, crumbling to the ground.

More than a dozen skull warriors still lurched across the graveyard that had been transformed into a battlefield. The Protectors were bracing themselves to attack the rest when the giant snake swept forward across the grass. The skull warriors stopped and turned to face the snake, just before it lifted the front of its long body and brought it down with a loud thump against the ground. To make sure the warriors wouldn't get up again, the snake rolled back and forth, driving the broken skeletons deeper into the earth.

"Nice work, pal," Nilkuu said to the snake.

Kivoda spotted a heap of broken bones on the far side of a tombstone and said, "Those remains look like they were broken recently, but we didn't make that mess."

"And look here," said Vizuna, pointing to another wide heap of bones and skulls that rested along the base of a wall. "There must have been an even bigger fight here earlier. Judging from the way the grass is bent around the bones, the fight happened less than an hour ago."

"If the skull warriors fought the Toa," said Nilkuu, "it looks like the Toa won!"

"Perhaps they went this way," said Izotor,

who stood at the edge of an ancient path that wound through the graveyard. He pointed to one of the graveyard's surrounding walls, where a section of the wall had collapsed.

Vizuna moved beside Izotor and dropped to a crouch. Examining the path, he said, "A lot of large footprints here. I don't see Toa Lewa's footprints, but then again, Lewa can fly."

"I've only seen Toa Kopaka's footprints in the snow before," Izotor said, "but those prints over there are definitely his. And all these prints lead toward that break in the wall."

"Let's follow them," said Kivoda.

The giant snake slithered after the Protectors and Harvali as they walked out of the graveyard and over the rubble of the collapsed wall. They proceeded up a street that was lined with stone structures. The only signs of life were the weeds that grew up from between the street's ancient paving stones, the vines that stretched over the structures' walls and roofs, and the wild trees that grew up through and around the structures.

The group moved up a hill and was approaching the remains of a town square when Harvali said, "If I remember the old maps correctly, we're near the tomb of Ekimu. The top of the building is decorated with a large stone sculpture of Ekimu's mask. We should see it around the next corner, on our right."

They turned the corner. Harvali gasped. The tomb of Ekimu was precisely where she had thought it would be, but the massive stone sculpture of Ekimu's mask had broken away from the building's roof, and now rested at an odd angle on the stairs that led up to the tomb. Several monstrously long and spindly legs jutted out from between the sculpture and the steps.

The large snake, which had been keeping close to Nilkuu, hissed at the sight of the monstrous legs. Nilkuu moved nearer to the legs to inspect them. "I don't know what evil creatures own those legs, but it looks like they got hit hard!"

Vizuna said, "Perhaps a Toa shoved the mask on top of them."

"Perhaps the Toa are inside the tomb now!" said Harvali. "Let's look."

The snake waited outside the building while the others climbed up the steps and entered through an open doorway. The tomb was decorated with numerous urns and statues that stood on pedestals. Moving carefully past the artefacts, the Protectors and Harvali soon found a large sarcophagus. The lid to the sarcophagus had been slid back to reveal a coffin.

The coffin was open. It was empty.

Harvali said, "Did someone break in and take Ekimu's body?"

"It doesn't look like it," Vizuna said. "Look at these marks in the dust inside and around the edges of the sarcophagus. The person inside the coffin *climbed* out."

"Then . . . Ekimu has risen!" Harvali said with obvious excitement.

"But where is he now?" said Korgot.

"And where are the Toa?" added Narmoto.

A muffled blast came from outside the tomb. Leaving the sarcophagus, the Protectors and Harvali ran outside, where they found the snake huddled against the side of the building, waiting for them. "The noise spooked the snake," Nilkuu said. "Where did the explosion come from?"

A second blast echoed across the city. Korgot said, "It came from there." She pointed to a tall, anvil-shaped structure that stood alone atop a hill. The structure's upper windows were brightly illuminated.

"That's the Forge of the Mask Makers," said Vizuna. "It's been sealed off for years."

"But someone's in it now," said Narmoto.

Another blast sounded, and simultaneously a brilliant burst of light radiated from the Forge's windows. Kivoda said, "There's a fight going on!"

"Stay here with the snake, Harvali," said Vizuna, "while we find out what's going on."

Without knowing whom or what they might encounter, the brave Protectors ran for the Forge as fast as they could. The Forge's front steps led up to a pair of heavy doors that had been blasted off their ancient hinges from the inside. The Protectors drew their weapons as they ran into the Forge.

They slowed down when they came upon a large, muscular beast lying on his back, motionless, on the floor. The creature had a sharp-horned head and no mask. He was still breathing, but his eyes stared blankly at the ceiling.

Passing a pair of towering columns, the Protectors proceeded into the Forge. They entered a large chamber that was lined with dust-covered shelves and containers that held precious metals and crystals. Numerous tools used for crafting masks lay across old worktables and benches that were also covered with dust. The Protectors were surprised to find another unconscious monster lying on the floor. The second monster also had a horned head and was without a mask.

Vizuna's eyes went wide as he saw the second monster. Before Vizuna or the other Protectors could ask whether the Toa were responsible for defeating both villains, they noticed more figures sprawled across the floor.

The Protectors suddenly realized that the other figures were the Toa. Pohatu, Onua, Tahu, Kopaka, Gali, and Lewa appeared to have been badly beaten.

Kivoda gasped. "Lewa's mask is gone."

"All the Toa's masks are gone," said Korgot. "Are they still alive?"

"Oh, they'll live," said a voice from behind the Protectors. They turned fast to see an individual clad in an ornate golden mask and armour. He carried a large hammer in one hand. He said, "If you came to join the fight, you're a bit late for that. But just so you know, the Toa won."

The Protectors dropped to their knees and bowed to Ekimu the Mask Maker.

CHAPTER 6

THE HEROES REUNITE

"It's good to see you again, my friends," said Ekimu as he gazed at the kneeling Protectors. "But please, get up off the floor, and let me have a good look at you."

The Protectors rose to their feet. Ekimu smiled behind his mask as he shook his head. "By the stars! Agarak, Udapo, Owa, Epolim, Kerato, and Mamuk, you've hardly changed at all."

Vizuna glanced at Narmoto, then looked

back to Ekimu and said, “Forgive me for saying so, Master Ekimu, but you’re mistaken. You see, those names you just said, well, those names belonged to our ancestors.”

Ekimu sighed. “You’re quite right, of course. It is I who should ask *you* for forgiveness. Seeing you here, standing before me, wearing the very same masks and armour that I crafted for the ancient Protectors, I simply forgot that thousands of years have passed. But you all have me at a disadvantage. You know my name, but I don’t know yours.”

After the Protectors identified themselves to Ekimu, he said, “I imagine you have a lot of questions, as do I. But first, help me carry the Toa on to the worktables that I’ve set up in the next room. Our timeless heroes don’t look very comfortable on the floor. I’ll tell you what happened while we move them.”

As the Protectors moved the Toa on to the

worktables, Ekimu said, "After thousands of years in a state of lifeless sleep, I awoke almost immediately when the Toa discovered me in my tomb. I quickly sensed an evil presence, and realized a creature under my evil breather's control, called Skull Grinder, had invaded my Forge. The Toa squabbled among themselves until they realized they needed to be united to defeat evil. They kept Skull Grinder and his servant Skull Basher occupied while I reassembled my Sacred Hammer of Power, which I used to subdue Skull Grinder. Unfortunately, Skull Grinder managed to knock the Masks of Power from the Toa's faces."

"Where are their masks now?" Narmoto said as he and Izotor lowered Tahu on to a table.

"Patience, Protector of Fire," said Ekimu. "I collected their masks and was restoring power to them just before you arrived. They should be ready now. Excuse me while I get them."

After Ekimu left the room, the Protectors heard Harvali call from a nearby corridor, “Hello? Protectors? Is everyone okay in there?”

Vizuna stepped out into the corridor, saw Harvali, and said, “This way.” He led Harvali into the room where the six maskless Toa were lying on the tables.

Seeing the Toa, Harvali trembled and said, “Are they all right?”

“Master Ekimu says they’ll be fine.”

“Ekimu?” Harvali gasped.

“We bowed to him,” Nilkuu said, “just like in the ancient reliefs. I told you we’d all survive!”

“I can’t believe that all this is happening,” Harvali said as she stepped towards the Toa. “I feel like . . . like I’m *living* history! I’m afraid I may faint.”

Ekimu was carrying a wide metal tray as he walked back into the room. The six Golden Masks of Power rested upon the tray. Seeing

Harvali, Ekimu said, "Well, hello! And who might you be?"

Harvali's head fell against her shoulder at the same instant that her legs buckled and she began to collapse. Nilkuu reached out and caught her before she fell.

"My goodness," said Narmoto. "She really did faint!"

"Her name is Harvali of the Jungle Region," said Vizuna as Nilkuu placed Harvali on to a spare worktable. "She's an archaeologist."

"An archaeologist?" said Ekimu. "After she wakes up, I imagine she and I shall have much to talk about!" Moving from one table to the next, he placed the Masks of Power over the faces of the Toa.

Energy began radiating from the Toa's masks. One by one, the heroes awoke and sat up. The Protectors moved closer to the Toa. Korgot said, "How do you feel, Onua?"

Onua, Master of Earth, rubbed the back of his head and said, "A bit woozy. But it's good to see you again, Korgot."

Tahu, Master of Fire, said, "What happened to Skull Grinder?"

Ekimu said, "Both Skull Grinder and Skull Basher remain knocked out. But just to stay on the safe side . . ." Ekimu gestured to a wall where two skull-like masks dangled from hooks. "Without their masks, they won't be going anywhere. Well, come along now, Toa. Get off those tables. We have much work to do! Our first order of business is to lock up Skull Grinder and Skull Basher where they can't hurt anyone."

After the Toa had transferred Skull Grinder and Skull Basher to separate vaults and locked them in securely, Ekimu continued, "The evil spirit of my brother, Makuta, hangs heavily in the air in the City of the Mask Makers. Indeed, his evil casts a shroud over our entire island. There are many ways to fight evil, and one way is to reclaim this city, to encourage islanders to live here again. We may never restore this city to its former glory, but we can do everything in our power to keep evil out!"

Kivoda said, "Master Ekimu, just so you know, the city's plumbing will need a good deal of repairs. The other Protectors and I encountered some trouble on the way here, and—"

"Trouble?" Ekimu interrupted. "What kind of trouble?"

"Well," Kivoda continued, "we entered the city through a series of underground caverns, where we found an army of skull spiders trying to heal the Lord of Skull Spiders after they'd hauled him up from the chasm. To make sure they didn't escape into the city or attack the Toa, we collapsed an entire cave on them."

"Well done, Protectors!" Ekimu said. "The Toa can learn from your example of working together."

"I'm glad you think so," Kivoda continued, "because . . . how shall I say this? The city's underground reservoirs aren't what they used to be."

Ekimu clapped a hand on Kivoda's shoulder and said, "No challenge is too great if we work together." He looked out through a window and saw that darkness had fallen. Turning away from the window, he darted over to a shelf and picked up two large boxes. "I suggest we all go outside. And wake up the archaeologist! She won't want to miss this." Taking the boxes with him, Ekimu headed for the corridor that led to an exit.

The other Protectors and the Toa followed Ekimu, but Vizuna and Nilkuu stepped over to Harvali, who was still stretched out on a worktable. Nilkuu said, “Harvali, can you hear me? You need to wake up. I think Master Ekimu has a surprise in store for us!”

“A surprise?” Harvali murmured as she opened her eyes. Looking from Nilkuu to Vizuna, she said, “So I wasn’t dreaming. We’re still in the Mask Maker’s Forge?”

“Yes,” Vizuna said, “but come along. Master Ekimu wants us outside.”

Vizuna and Nilkuu helped Harvali off the table and kept close to her as they guided her out of the building. “Thanks for watching out for me,” Harvali said, “but you can relax now. I don’t think I’ll faint again.”

They found their allies standing in a grassy courtyard behind the Forge. The giant snake had joined the group, and had slithered to rest in the grass nearby. Ekimu had already emptied the boxes of their contents, and Vizuna saw that the Mask Maker was now busy positioning a cylindrical projectile to the side of a rickety-looking tripod.

Harvali said, "What is it?"

"An old rocket launcher," Vizuna said.

"It looks *thousands* of years old," Harvali said.

"It *is* thousands of years old!" said Ekimu. "Fortunately, I built this thing to last!"

The Toa, the Protectors and Harvali cautiously backed away from Ekimu. But then Ekimu turned to Tahu and Narmoto and said, "Master of Fire and Protector of Fire! Will you please do the honours?" He gestured to a long fuse that extended from the bottom of the rocket.

Tahu and Narmoto stepped over to the rocket launcher and snapped their fingers, producing small balls of fire at the ends of their fingertips. They extended their fingers towards the fuse, watched it ignite, and then moved back from the launcher.

The fuse hissed loudly as it burned, prompting the giant snake to lift its head and hiss back. A shower of sparks erupted from the rocket's base, and the projectile leaped into the night sky, leaving a blazing trail in its wake.

The rocket exploded, spraying brilliant fireworks in all directions. The fireworks swerved away from one another before they regrouped, blazing brightly as they appeared to dance in broad circles, high above the city. The giant snake cringed as the fireworks whizzed and popped loudly overhead.

Ekimu looked at the Toa, then gestured to them, saying, "That display could use a boost, so everyone on the island can see the fireworks. Let's show every islander that this city is once again open to the public!"

The Toa arranged themselves in a circle around Ekimu as they lifted their gazes to the sky. Elemental energy flowed from their masks, and rose up like a wave to push the fireworks higher, and then higher still. And as the fireworks continued to dance and twirl, they grew even brighter.

Vizuna looked at Korgot and saw that she was gazing up at the fireworks. He moved beside her and said, "Is now a good time to remind you that you wanted to ask me something?"

"Sure," Korgot said. "I was wondering if you could show me how to use your flame bow. I've always wanted to try it. And if you're curious to test out my star drill I'd be glad to teach you."

Vizuna nodded agreeably. "Perhaps all the Protectors should learn to handle one another's weapons. In the event of an emergency, such knowledge would be useful!"

"Are you sure this rope bridge will hold?" said Ekimu.

"I'm sure," said Harvali. "I supervised its construction, and I trust the builders with my life!"

They were standing with the Protectors at the edge of the City of the Mask Makers, at the site of the collapsed bridge, where a new rope bridge extended across the chasm. Using ropes, vines, and salvaged wooden planks from throughout the city, the Protectors and the Toa had worked through the night to build the bridge. Lewa had made multiple flights back and forth over the chasm, hauling the ropes from one side of the bridge to the other, and making sure the anchors on both sides were secure.

Overhearing Ekimu's question, Korgot said, "The bridge is definitely sturdy, Master Ekimu. Onua is the heaviest Toa, and he's already walked across it four times."

Ekimu sighed. "I miss the old bridge, but it did have certain structural problems. With a bit of training, the Toa should be able to focus their Masks of Power in combination with my own Mask of Creation to build a bridge that's even more durable than the one that stood here for eons."

"In the meantime," Nilkuu said, "this rope bridge will allow the new colonists to enter the city. And look! Here they come now!"

The group gazed across the chasm, where hundreds of islanders walked along a ridge, approaching the rope bridge. Even across the distance, the Protectors could sense the islanders' excitement as they neared the bridge's gateway, where the six Toa waited to greet them.

"Today is a glorious day," said Narmoto.

"One for the history books!" said Harvali.

"But remember," Ekimu said, "so long as there is evil on Okoto, we must all stay vigilant."

Kivoda said, "Master Ekimu, do you have any special instructions for the colonists after they arrive?"

"Yes," Ekimu said. "Tell them that we should all meet in the city's main square this evening. Because tonight, we shall rejoice with even greater fireworks!"

As the Protectors greeted the new arrivals, Ekimu felt a cold chill travel down his back, so cold that he turned to look behind him. Although he saw nothing unusual, he sensed an evil presence. Closing his eyes, he thought, *I know you're out there, Makuta. I know you're waiting to strike again. But when you do, I shall be prepared to strike back!*